Jean Little

Wishes

illustrated by
Geneviève Côté

North Winds Press
An Imprint of Scholastic Canada Ltd.

The illustrations for this book were created in mixed media.
The type was set in 24 point ITC Esprit.

Library and Archives Canada Cataloguing in Publication
Little, Jean, 1932-
Wishes / by Jean Little ; illustrations by Geneviève Côté.

ISBN 978-1-4431-0772-3

I. Côté, Geneviève, 1964- II. Title.

PS8523.I77W57 2012   jC813'.54   C2012-901577-6

6 5 4 3 2 1   Printed in Singapore 46   12 13 14 15 16

For Lisa and Raymah, with our love.
— J.L.

For Yan — impeccable sense of timing!
— G.C.

If wishes were horses,
then poor folks would ride.

If wishes were friendships,
I'd be by your side.

If wishes were flowers,
I'd get Mom a rose
with velvety petals
to tickle her nose.

4

If wishes were sundaes,
I'd split a banana.

If wishes were kisses,
I'd give mine to Nana.

If wishes were puppies,
my brother would get
a puppy called Snug
for his personal pet.

If wishes were skylarks,
the sky would be singing.

If wishes were ball games,
my bat would be swinging.

If wishes were ice cream,
our cones would be doubles.

If wishes were soapsuds,
we'd blow shining bubbles.

If wishes were rowboats,
I'd take my dad fishing
and we'd catch our supper
with no need for wishing.

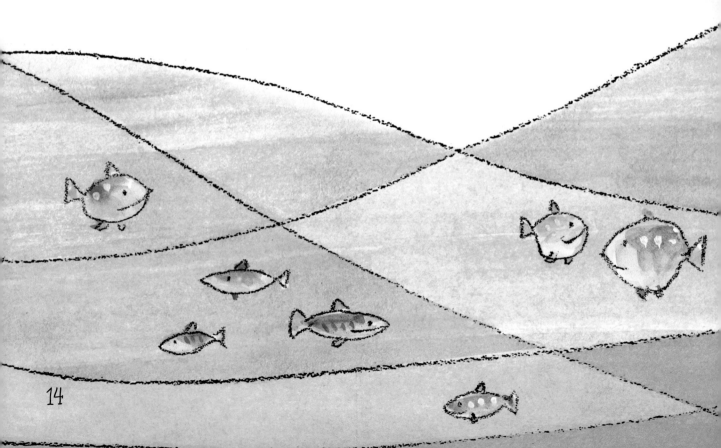

If wishes were snowflakes,
we'd hurry outside
and make great snow angels
with wings spreading wide.

If wishes were pancakes,
I'd eat a tall stack.

If wishes were parsnips,
I'd send the plate back.

If wishes could grant me
a time travel journey,
I'd live in a castle
and joust in a tourney.

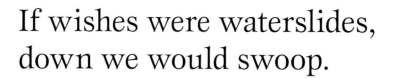

If wishes were waterslides,
down we would swoop.

If wishes were wings,
we would go loop-the-loop.

23

If wishes were trampolines,
I'd practise flips.

If wishes were fishes,
I'd have mine with chips.

If wishes were circuses,
I'd be a clown
with a bulging red nose
and my pants falling down.

I'd try for a handstand
and land on my rear
and the grown-ups would groan
and the children would cheer.

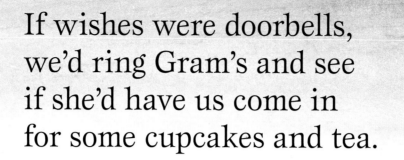

If wishes were doorbells,
we'd ring Gram's and see
if she'd have us come in
for some cupcakes and tea.

And we would swap stories
and sing songs and laugh…

29

and she'd ask us to stay
for a week and a half.